ABOUT THE BANK STREET READY-TO-READ SERIES

Seventy years of educational research and innovative teaching have given the Bank Street College of Education the reputation as America's most trusted name in early childhood education.

Because no two children are exactly alike in their development, we have designed the *Bank Street Ready-to-Read* series in three levels to accommodate the individual stages of reading readiness of children ages four through eight.

- *Level 1:* GETTING READY TO READ—read-alouds for children who are taking their first steps toward reading.
- *Level 2:* READING TOGETHER—for children who are just beginning to read by themselves but may need a little help.
- *Level 3:* I CAN READ IT MYSELF—for children who can read independently.

Our three levels make it easy to select the books most appropriate for a child's development and enable him or her to grow with the series step by step. The *Bank Street Ready-to-Read* books also overlap and reinforce each other, further encouraging the reading process.

We feel that making reading fun and enjoyable is the single most important thing that you can do to help children become good readers. And we hope you'll be a part of Bank Street's long tradition of learning through sharing.

The Bank Street College of Education

To Linda Greengrass
— W.H.H., J.O., B.B.

For John Massimino
— D.C.

HOW DO YOU MAKE A BUBBLE?
A Bantam Little Rooster Book / May 1992

Little Rooster is a trademark of Bantam Books, a division of
Bantam Doubleday Dell Publishing Group, Inc.

Series graphic design by Alex Jay / Studio J

Special thanks to James A. Levine and Betsy Gould.

Library of Congress Cataloging-in-Publication Data

Hooks, William H.
How do you make a bubble? / by William H. Hooks;
illustrated by Doug Cushman.
p.   cm. — (Bank Street ready-to-read)
"A Byron Preiss Book."
"A Bantam little rooster book."
Summary: This simple rhyming text poses questions
about how to do a variety of things
and provides the answers.
ISBN 0-553-07887-9. — ISBN 0-553-35487-6 (pbk.)
[1. Stories in rhyme.]   I. Cushman, Doug, ill.
II. Title.   III. Series.
PZ8.3.H765Ho   1992
[E] — dc20
91-467   CIP   AC

Published simultaneously in the United States and Canada

PRINTED IN THE UNITED STATES OF AMERICA

0 9 8 7 6 5 4 3 2 1

Bank Street Ready-to-Read™

How Do You Make a Bubble?

by William H. Hooks, Joanne
Oppenheim, and Barbara Brenner
Illustrated by Doug Cushman

A Byron Preiss Book

A BANTAM LITTLE ROOSTER BOOK
NEW YORK · TORONTO · LONDON · SYDNEY · AUCKLAND

How do you make a pie?
You bake it.

How do you make a malted?
You shake it.

How do you make a pancake?
You flip it.

How do you drink a soda?
You sip it.

How do you make a poem?
You write it.

How do you eat an apple?
You bite it.

How do you make a scarf?
You knit it.

How do you play a drum?
You hit it.

How do you make a bow?
You tie it.

How do you sail a kite?
You fly it.

How do you make a fire?
You light it.

How do you fix a wrong?
You right it.

How do you make a picture?
You draw it.

How do you eat a bone?
You gnaw it.

How do you take a photo?
You shoot it.

How do you blow a horn?
You toot it.

How do you make a necklace?
You string it.

How do you throw a Frisbee?
You fling it.

How do you make a tower?
You stack it.

How do you break an egg?
You crack it.

How do you make a bubble?
You blow it.

How do you pitch a ball?
You throw it.

How do you make a snack?
You pop it.

How do you feed a pig?
You slop it.

How do you water the grass?
You hose it.

How do you smell a flower?
You nose it.

How do you make this book end?
You close it.

Together and individually, William H. Hooks, Barbara Brenner, and Joanne Oppenheim have written over one hundred books for children. Before creating the Bank Street Ready-to-Read series, they helped pioneer the well-known Bank Street Readers, the nation's first beginning reader series specifically geared toward multicultural urban audiences. Mr. Hooks currently lives in Chapel Hill, North Carolina, Ms. Brenner in Hawley, Pennsylvania, and Ms. Oppenheim in Monticello, New York.

Doug Cushman is the author and illustrator of many children's books, including *Possum Stew, Camp Big Paw,* and *Aunt Eater Loves a Mystery,* a *Reading Rainbow* selection. Mr. Cushman lives in East Haven, Connecticut, with his wife, illustrator Kim Mulkey.